For Emily
and Sarah

The Standard Publishing Company, Cincinnati, Ohio
A division of Standex International Corporation
© 1993 by The Standard Publishing Company
All rights reserved.
Printed in the United States of America
00 99 98 97 96 95 94 93   5 4 3 2 1

ISBN 0-7847-0063-X
Cataloging-in-Publication data available
Designed by Coleen Davis

Scriptures taken from the following versions: From the International Children's Bible, New Century Version, © 1986, 1988 by Word Publishing, Dallas, Texas 75039. Used by permission. From the HOLY BIBLE—NEW INTERNATIONAL VERSION, © 1973, 1978, 1984 by the International Bible Society. Used by permission of Zondervan Bible Publishers. From The Bible in Today's English Version, © 1966, 1971, 1976 by the American Bible Society. Used by permission. From the Revised Standard Version of the Bible, © 1946, 1952.

- An -
A•B•C CHRISTMAS

written by **Amy Houts**

illustrated by **Nancy Munger**

LITTLE DEER BOOKS
PSALM 42:1

Standard Publishing
Cincinnati, Ohio

Aa angel

God sent the angel Gabriel to a town in Galilee.

Luke 1:26

Bb baby

The baby will be holy.

Luke 1:35

Cc carols

I will sing praises to my God.

Psalm 104:33

Dd dream

An angel of the Lord came to Joseph in a dream.

Matthew 1:20

Ee earth

Glory to God and peace on earth!

Luke 2:14

Ff flocks

There were shepherds keeping watch over their flocks.

Luke 2:8

Gg good news

of
Great
JOY
for all people.

Luke 2:10

Good news of great joy for all the people.
Luke 2:10

Hh heavenly host

A multitude of the heavenly host praising God.

Luke 2:13

Ii inn

There was no room for them in the inn.

Luke 2:7

Jj Jesus

You will name him Jesus.

Matthew 1:21

Kk King

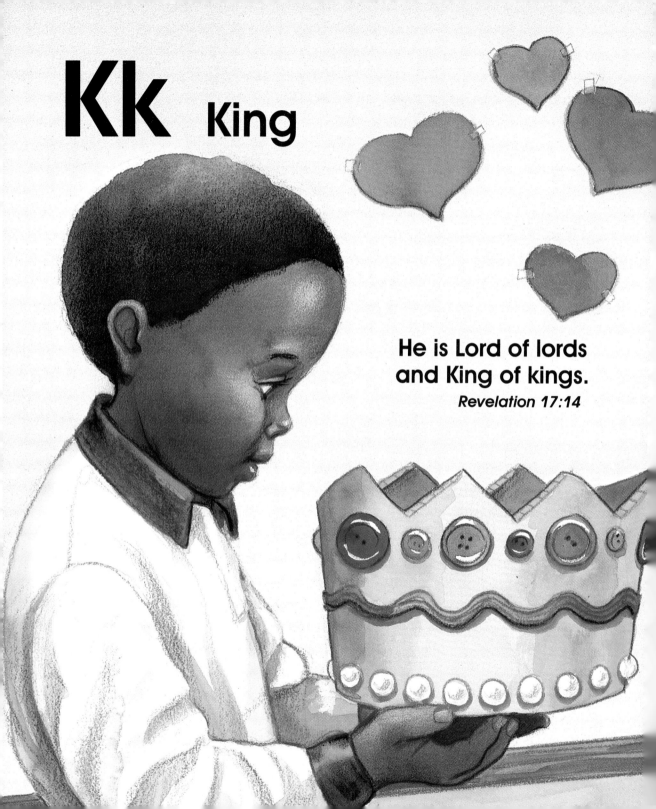

He is Lord of lords
and King of kings.
Revelation 17:14

Ll love

**God loved the world so much
that he gave his only Son.**

John 3:16

Mm manger

She wrapped him in swaddling cloths and laid him in a manger.

Matthew 2:7

Nn Nazareth

Joseph went from the town of Nazareth to Bethlehem.

Luke 2:4

Oo ornaments
The wings of a dove covered with silver.

Psalm 68:1

Pp praise

The shepherds went back to their sheep, praising God.

Luke 2:20

Qq quilt

God's glory will cover and protect the whole city.

Isaiah 4:5

Rr remember

Mary remembered all these things.

Luke 2:19

Ss star

We have seen his star
in the East.

Matthew 2:2

Tt treasures

They gave him treasures of gold, frankincense, and myrrh.

Matthew 2:11

Uu us

Let us go to Bethlehem and see.

Luke 2:15

Vv very

**This very day your Savior
was born—Christ the Lord!**
Luke 2:11

Ww wise men

Wise men from the east came to Jerusalem.

Matthew 2:7

Xx Yy Zz

zzzzz . . . .

Dreaming of that long ago night in Bethlehem.